no rest for edwin

by
marc tetro

Thanks Liane Morrisette for your wit and your ideas. To my family and friends for their help and support: A.D. Walter and Shirley Tomiak, Darryl Horeczy, Raymond and Louise Tetreault, Laurent Tetreault, Bob Tetreault and Pierre Côté. Thank you Dale.

Illustrations, Text and Design © 1998 Marc Tetro

Story Concept: Carolynn Pawluk.

First published in Canada by
McArthur & Company
322 King Street West, Suite 402, Toronto, Ontario, Canada M5V 1J2

Canadian Cataloguing in Publication Data

Tetro, Marc, 1960-
No rest for Edwin

ISBN 1-55278-008-2

I. Title

PS8589.E884N62 1998   jC813'.54   C98-931676-9
PZ7.T47No 1998

Printing and bindery: Transcontinental Printing

Printed in Canada

(LOOK JUST around)
THE Tree

as THE FiRST SnoWFLaKeS OF WinTer FeLL OUTSiDe THeir Den, THe moTHer Bear Said To Her CUBS,

'Come on KiDS, LeT'S GeT reaDy For BeD. iT'S Time To HiBernaTe For THe winTer.'

So one BY one THe CUBS PrePareD For THeir LonG winTer SLeeP.

all except one.
edwin didn't want
to sleep, this was his first
winter, and he wanted to play
in the snow.
'why do we have to hibernate,
mom?' he asked.

'it saves our energy so that
we can be strong and healthy
in the spring.'

but edwin already felt strong
and healthy. he had energy to
spare, and he wanted to see
what winter was like.

SO, very early in the morning, when everyone was asleep, edwin snuck out of the den to see his first winter.

THE FOREST WAS COVERED
WITH A BEAUTIFUL
BLANKET OF SNOW.

EDWIN LOVED
THE SNOW
BUT WHAT HE REALLY
WANTED WAS SOMEONE
TO PLAY WITH.

INSIDE A BIG TREE
HE FOUND A FAMILY
OF SQUIRRELS
NESTLED TOGETHER
SNOOZING.

'WHAT are YOU DOING awake?'
Said one of THEM.
'YOU SHOULD BE SLEEPING-CAN'T YOU
See it's winter?' 'I want TO PLaY!'
BUT THE SQUIRRELS JUST YawneD
and WENT BaCK TO SLeep.

Just around the tree
Edwin heard a sound.
Some Boys were
PLAying Hockey!
Edwin was Fascinated!!
IT Looked Like so
much Fun! He wanted
To Try iT Too. So when the
Boys went in To warm up,
Edwin Snuck out
From Behind the Tree.

He picked up the skates, sat down and tried to put them on.

He struggled a bit to get his paws in, and he had some trouble with the laces, but finally he got them both on.

Then he tried to stand up...

WHOa!

THiS was Harder
THan iT LOOKeD !

AFTER SEVERAL ATTEMPTS EDWIN FINALLY GOT HIS BALANCE.

AND BEFORE HE KNEW IT, HE WAS SKATING!

EDWIN WAS HAVING SO MUCH FUN HE DIDN'T EVEN NOTICE THE BOYS STANDING AT THE EDGE OF THE RINK.

THE BOYS GAVE
EDWIN A STICK AND
EXPLAINED THE
RULES,

BUT IT TOOK a WHILE
FOR eDWiN TO
FiGUre THinGS OUT.

every time someone passed the puck his way, he would drop his stick and try to catch it, sometimes throwing his whole body on it or batting it right out of the air.

'no, no! You're supposed
to use your stick!'

but edwin just couldn't
get the hang of it.

HE WAS GOOD AT STOPPING THE PUCK THOUGH!

One Time He even STOPPED iT WITH HiS HEAD. IT MADE HIM a LITTLE DIZZY, SO HE DECIDED NOT TO TRY THAT aGain.

FINALLY THE BOYS DECIDED THAT THE BEST POSITION FOR EDWIN WOULD BE GOALIE.

AND WHAT A GREAT GOALIE HE MADE!

He didn't let a single shot through all afternoon. It seemed that nothing could get by edwin's big paws.

THEY PLAYED AND PLAYED
UNTIL THE AFTERNOON
CAME AND WENT.
BY DINNERTIME, EDWIN WAS
HUNGRY AND READY FOR A NAP.

HE STRUGGLED OUT OF
HIS SKATES AND SAID GOODBYE
TO HIS NEW FRIENDS.

WHeN He arriveD HoMe, HiS moTHer was in a panic.
'WHere Have You Been? i've Been worrieD sick!'

eDwiN LOOKeD up aT Her wiTH weary eyes anD saiD 'i'm sorry mom'.

THen He cLiMBeD inTO BeD wiTH THe oTHer cuBS for a GOOD niGHT'S reST.

BUT WHEN MORNING CAME, EDWIN DIDN'T WAKE UP. HE WAS SO TIRED HE DIDN'T WAKE UP THE MORNING AFTER THAT, EITHER.

INSTEAD, HE JUST SLEPT AND SLEPT, DREAMING OF ICE SKATES AND HOCKEY AND OF HIS NEW FRIENDS,